The Three Robots
And The Sandstorm

by
Art Fettig

Illustrated by Joe Carpenter

Dedicated to all of the
"Pos" people in this
wonderful world.

Published by

GROWTH UNLIMITED, INC.
Dedicated to creating positive living concepts for children.

31 EAST AVE SOUTH
BATTLE CREEK, MICHIGAN 49017

Manufactured in the United States of America
Layout and Type by A-Z Typesetting

Library of Congress Catalog Card Number 82-090993
Fettig, Art
The Three Robots and the Sand Storm
ISBN 0-9601334-3-7
2 3 4 5 6 7 8 9 0

The windy season has come to the land of Tomorrow.
And our friends, the Three Robots, were gathered together
in the park early that morning to sing their happiness song.

3

Neg, the smallest of the three, seemed to have the loudest voice when they sang together. It wasn't unusual at all for him to get so happy and enthusiastic during their singing, that the light on top of his head would light up with a bright ray which could be seen even in the morning sunshine.

4

Semi-Pos really looked forward to these daily meetings too. It was a good time for him to remind himself that he still had those old words in the back of his mind, the words "put it off", "tomorrow", "not now", "mañana" and "when I get around to it!" And only by strengthening his positive attitude every day was he able to remain positive in his thoughts and actions.

put it off
tomorrow
not now
mañana
when I get around to it

Neg understood this too, and perhaps that was why he worked so hard at keeping happy thoughts in his mind. He remembered the pain he had felt every day when his mind was filled with the words "can't", "don't", "frown" and "never". Neg never wanted to have that unhappy feeling again.

Life was just too wonderful to ever want to go back to the old way of thinking.

6

Pos was more fortunate than the other Robots, because the words in her mind were all positive. The screen on the back of her head displayed words like — "can", "will", "smile", "happy" and "can do."

But Pos knew that unless she worked on her thinking every day, negative words could find their way onto her screen. After all, there were negative ideas everywhere. The newspapers were full of bad news and so were the TV screens and the radio news broadcasts. It would seem that people believed the only news worth telling was bad news. If only those people who gathered the news could look for the positive side, what a happier world this would be.

7

Pos certainly enjoyed her morning visit with her friends — Semi-Pos and Neg, and she really loved to join them in their morning singing sessions.

The robots had greeted each other this morning with bright smiles and kind words, and now they had joined hands and it was Neg this morning who led the singing — he sang the introduction to their song. And now all three robots sang together in beautiful harmony.

The Robots had no sooner finished their singing when they heard the roaring, frightening sound of an on rushing wind.

They were accustomed to winds, but this one sounded stronger and louder than any wind they'd ever heard before. Without warning, the wind had come on with such sudden force that it blew them along.

Soon they were separated from each other, falling, flying, rolling and spinning, unable to do anything about where they went or how. The wind howled and roared, and then it left as quickly as it had come. Now it was very quiet, and Neg came tumbling to a sudden stop. He shook his head. Slowly he opened one eye and then the other. He was stunned. Groggy, he felt a sudden lack of energy. Neg was confused. And then he realized that he was alone.

10

He turned his head to the right to look for his friends, and discovered that his head did not want to turn the way it normally did. It turned almost not at all and he could sense a gritty sound.

The sand. Now he remembered that this was no ordinary wind. It was a wind filled with sand, and although he had tried to protect his body from the blast, the wind was just too strong for him.

Now he understood the problem. There was sand in his neck and his head simply would not turn correctly.

Meanwhile, Pos had an even greater concern. Her right leg would not move at all. Every joint was locked in place. Her ankle would not bend at all; nor would her knee, and even the socket at the top of her leg was frozen stiff. Sand had worked its way into all of the joints of her leg and had frozen them in place.

Semi-Pos was suffering from a similar problem, but
with Semi-Pos it was his right arm. It, too, was locked up
tight and would not move.

The robots had been blown about so far and wide that they were blocks apart and could not help each other. Of course they tried. They cried as loudly as they could, but not quite loud enough for each to hear the others. One by one they recovered their senses and their strength, and struggled on alone in search of help.

Pos made it into a robot repair station first, and
after hours of waiting in a long line, the technician finally
completed her examination. She shook her head sadly
and then proceeded to give Pos the news.

"I'm sorry, your leg has sand in the joints, and already there is some permanent damage. We'll have to order a whole new right leg replacement."

"Well, then," Pos said as cheerfully as she could , "I'll just have to stumble along on this one."

"Oh, no!" the technician warned, "That would be impossible. If you carried that damaged leg around with you it would throw all of your other parts out of adjustment. We will have to take off your damaged leg and you must go without it until the replacement arrives."

Pos simply could not believe what she was hearing. "Go without a leg?" she asked. "How would I walk with only one leg? It would be impossible. Surely you have a spare leg you could loan me."

The technician threw up her hands in despair. "We don't have a spare part left. That sand storm damaged most of our population. And now the assembly plants will have to work overtime for months before things get back to normal."

And so, a few hours later, Pos, now minus her right leg, hobbled out of the repair shop. As she hopped on her remaining leg she tried bravely to catch her balance with a pair of crutches that the technician had provided. She fell. And once up, it took all of her courage to struggle on.

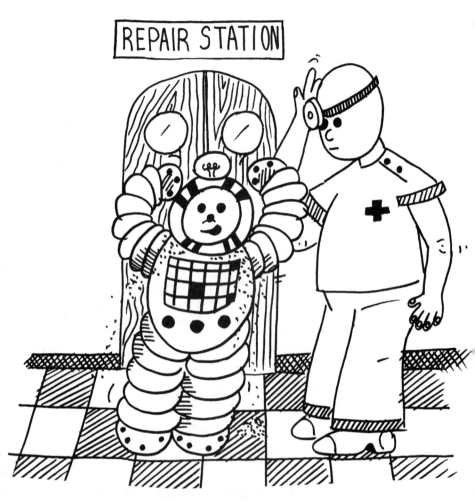

It was hours later when Neg finally worked his way to the front of the line at the Robot Repair Station.

By now his head was locked solid in a straight forward position. He could no longer move it up or down, or to the right or left.

"All it needs is a little oil — or maybe a spray of grease," he suggested.

But when the technician completed his exam he sadly explained to Neg that the sand in his neck had caused severe permanent damage and the only remedy would be replacement with a whole new neck assembly.

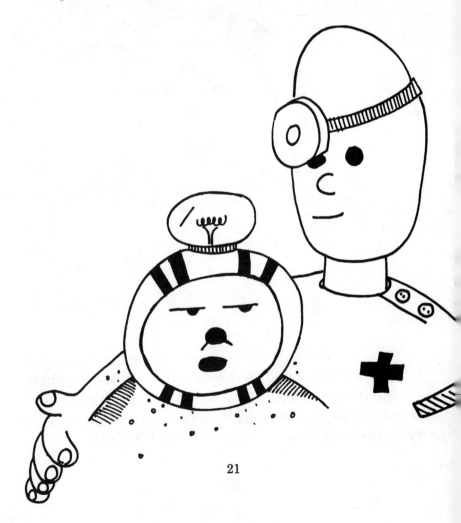

21

Neg would have to be satisfied to look straight ahead with no neck movement for a month, or possibly even longer, for as long as it might take until a new neck might be completed at the busy assembly plant.

If Neg could have turned his head to his right as he walked from the Robot Repair center, he would have seen his friend, Semi-Pos, still in line waiting for attention. As it was, he went walking right on by. And Semi-Pos was so busy looking at his stiff right arm that he too missed seeing his friend, Neg, as he walked by.

Two hours later Semi-Pos walked out through the doorway of the repair center minus his right arm at the shoulder joint. He too must go without, until a suitable replacement could be assembled.

As the robots struggled home that evening, each worried about the other two. Were they safe? How had they come through that terrible storm? Would they be there for the meeting tomorrow?

As morning came, Pos, Semi-Pos and Neg each felt doubts about their ability to attend the daily meeting in the park.

Neg had spent the whole night awake, tossing and turning in his bed, trying to find a way to be comfortable. His stiff neck made comfort impossible.

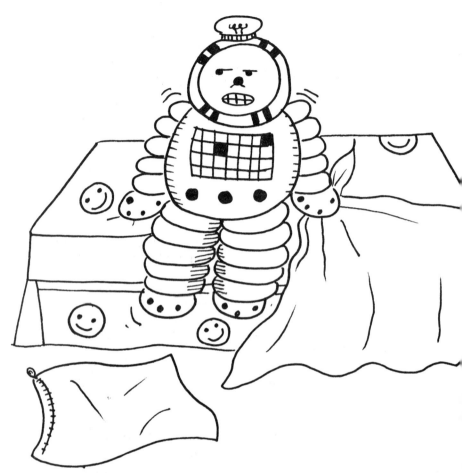

   As he slowly climbed out of bed, he tested his body.
He tried to turn his head to the right, but it remained
rigidly in place. He took a deep breath just in case there
might be pain. And he tried to turn his head to the left.
It did not turn. Now he tried to look up at the ceiling,
but it was as if his head were frozen solid in one position.
He could not move his head right or left or up or down.

Of course, his eyes still moved normally and as he tested his mobility he found that he could still move freely at the waist. So, he was not helpless! He could still get out of bed and walk about, but it was not at all normal having a neck that would not move.

Neg hoped that his friends would not make fun of him when they saw how his neck was locked in place. He walked slowly to the park that morning. He definitely had a problem looking straight ahead.

At one point he tripped over a shrub that he certainly knew was there. But because he could not look up and down normally, he missed it, and he reeled and tumbled to the ground. As he sat there he didn't know whether to laugh or cry. One big tear came to his eye but he quickly brushed it aside and forced a smile to his lips.

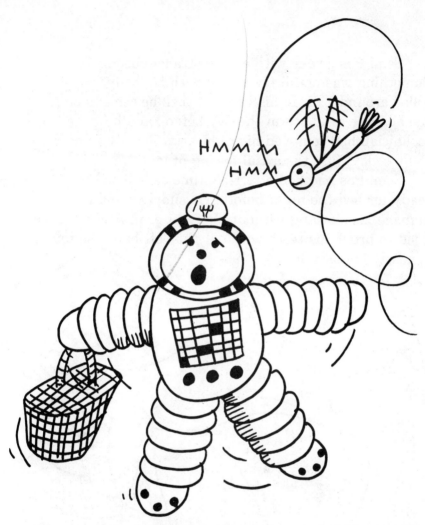

His stiff neck seemed to throw his whole balance off center and it took extra effort for him to get back to his feet. But Neg just tried harder, and soon he had himself pointed in the right direction, walking onward to the daily meeting with his friends in the park.

Semi-Pos awoke with a very strange feeling. Something was definitely wrong with his body. He slowly rolled around a bit in his bed and then he remembered the horrible sand storm the day before, and how the technician had removed his right arm. There was no pain there today, just the awful feeling of loss.

Semi-Pos had had a terrible time as he tried to get ready for bed the night before. He simply could not manage his clothing without his right arm. And when he tried to brush his teeth with only his left hand, he found it nearly impossible.

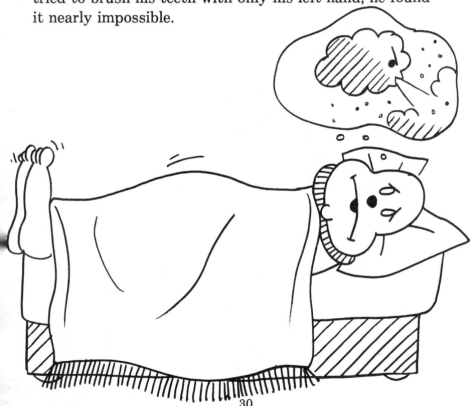

This morning he struggled once again. Instead of trying to put the toothpaste on his brush he tried to squeeze a little out in the wash basin and then when he had completed that task, he maneuvered the paste onto his brush.

Semi-Pos quickly discovered that a simple task like brushing his teeth in the morning is a major undertaking with just one hand. Especially his left hand when he was in the habit of using his right hand for most one handed tasks.

He knew he was a few minutes late as he rushed along the lane leading to their regular meeting place in the park.

Meanwhile, Pos was having an awful time. She had suffered so throughout the night, not from actual pain but from the pain of worry. "How can I possibly get by with only one leg?" she thought, and the more she worried about the idea, the worse she felt.

Pos had always been a healthy, happy, successful robot. She always wore a smile. She had always had positive, successful thoughts in her mind and now with one leg missing, Pos simply did not know what to think.

She was very tired as she got out of bed and prepared to go to meet her friends in the park. She was more than tired. She was weary.

As she stumbled out of bed, she did not notice the book that was lying on the floor. As she tried to swing up onto her foot she tripped on the book and went stumbling to the floor.

Pos just sat there on the floor for several moments feeling very very helpless. And then she tried to shake the feeling off as she struggled bravely to get up.

She made it all the way up and then, just as she
reached for her crutches, she tripped again and fell.

It was just too much for her and she sat half way up
and rested her head against her bed. A tear came to one
eye and then one came to the other, then a mass of tears
came gushing out and Pos just sat there and cried and
cried and cried.

Pos did not know what to do. For the first time in her life, Pos was a truly unhappy robot.

As Semi-Pos arrived at the bench in the park for the daily meeting he found that his friends were not in sight.

"What happened to my friends?" he thought. Then, of course, he started imagining horrible things.

He sat down on the bench and put his chin into his left hand for some serious worrying. His eyes came to rest on the trunk of a nearby tree. He thought he had seen someone duck behind the tree, but now no one was in sight.

He watched the tree and in a moment he saw it again. There was someone hiding there behind the tree and Semi-Pos called out with a brave voice, "Who is it? I see you behind that tree. Who is it? Come on out!"

Nothing happened. Semi-Pos waited a full minute and then he called out once more. "I see you there. Come on out."

Slowly a figure emerged. It was Neg. He was walking very slowly, as if he were shy, or possibly afraid of something. He was not acting normal at all. He held his head funny.

"What is it Neg?" Semi-Pos called as he ran to meet his friend. "What is wrong, Neg?"

Neg explained to his friend how horrible it was to have a stiff neck that would not allow him to move his head to the left or the right or up or down. He completely overlooked the fact that Semi-Pos was missing his right arm.

"Where is Pos?" Neg asked. Before Semi-Pos could reply, Neg asked, "Didn't she come? Is there something wrong with her? Where is she?"

43

The two robots sat there together, worrying about their friend Pos. An hour passed, and then two. They tried to start their meeting without her.

Twice Semi-Pos tried to start The Happiness Song. "We are happy, we're healthy, we're somebody ..." But that was as far as they could get in their song, because they were not happy at all. The two robots were very, very worried about their friend Pos.

At last they went home to rest.

44

Somehow the day had passed for the three robots, and now the night had passed too.

It was morning and again time for their morning meeting in the park.

Semi-Pos was there a minute or two late this morning, for he was still having a horrible time trying to live without a right hand. Neg was there early. He felt a little better because he had made the whole trip to the park without tripping over a single shrub.

46

The two robots waited, hoping that Pos would be there any moment. But as one hour passed and then two they knew — that something awful had happened to their friend Pos, and they must do something to find their friend.

47

Although the robots were good friends, they always met in the park, and strange as it may seem, none of them knew exactly where the other lived. "How could we find Pos?" they asked one another. Finally, after much thought, Neg came up with a suggestion. "We'll try the police."

As they walked to the police station together Semi-Pos discovered that if he put his left arm around Neg he could keep his balance much better. Being without a right arm threw his whole weight off balance.

Neg quickly discovered that Semi-Pos could help him see the shrubs and other obstacles better, and by walking as a team, they were both better off.

50

The trip to the police station was not successful. Nobody there knew Pos. She had never been in trouble and so she had had no experience with the police.

Semi-Pos and Neg were really concerned. Where
could they look for help to find their friend?

"What about the repair station?" Neg asked.
"Didn't we have to fill out a record with our names and addresses when we went through the station?"

"Sure we did." Semi-Pos replied.

The two robots rushed down the street together.
They were traveling much better now. Their disabilities
were easier to live with when they worked together.
When they arrived at the repair station, they were happy
to discover that the long lines had disappeared.

Quickly the aide checked the records for them, and
within a few minutes they found Pos' address.

It was just a few blocks from the repair station, and the two robots walked quickly at first, but their anxiety for their friend's safety grew as they got closer, and they actually ran the last hundred yards.

55

First, they tried the bell and when that didn't work,
Neg pounded loudly on the door.

56

It was just a minute, but to the two worried robots standing on the porch, it seemed more like an eternity.

57

Pos was in bed feeling very sad and alone, when she heard the doorbell ringing. She tried to get to her feet, but with the one leg missing, she failed the first time she tried. Then, when the loud knocking on the door began, she tried again, and then once again, and with several brave efforts she finally made it across the room to her crutches.

It took all her strength to make it across the room on her crutches to the front door. She nearly fell to the floor again. Catching herself at the last instant, she swung the door open.

"Pos!" Neg cried out. "We're so happy to see you. We missed you at the park."

Pos invited her friends indoors, and as Pos listened to her friends talk about their problems, she soon became less concerned with her own.

"I just couldn't walk to the park," Pos explained. "I felt so helpless and alone."

Neg laughed. "I was hiding behind the tree when Semi-Pos found me. I was afraid that you both would laugh at me because I could not turn my head."

Suddenly they all felt better. After a bit of
experimenting, the robots found that by depending on
one another, working as a team, they could walk down
the street together at a good pace.

There was Pos in the middle with her two arms around her friends, with Semi-Pos to her left, with his good arm swinging beside him. Neg was on her right, and the other two robots kept a sharp eye out to keep him out of trouble caused by his stiff neck.

With a little practice, they were soon getting into the rhythm of moving together. Neg was the first to break into a big smile of joy.

The other robots saw his smile. Semi-Pos was next. Then Pos caught the happy spirit and they hadn't walked a block together until Pos could no longer hold back the happiness that was returning to her life.

"Let's sing it fellows," she said. What a wonderful
sight it was to see, three helpful friends and what a
wonderful sound their sharing song was!

66

The three happy robots were walking along the street.

Pos was hopping along on one leg depending on her
friends for support.

Semi-Pos was swinging his left arm, and feeling so much better since Pos had promised to help him brush his teeth.

And Neg, was staring straight ahead, knowing that his friends would serve as his lookouts to keep him out of trouble.

The three happy robots were laughing together and
singing. Perhaps just a bit off key, but so loudly and so
merrily that it didn't matter.

The air was filled with the music of the song they
sang —

"We're happy.
We're healthy.
We're somebody!
Not a sad nobody.
No, we're somebody.

And we wear a smile.''

Pos felt wonderful. It was a new feeling, because although she was usually a happy robot, now happiness had a deeper meaning. Now she knew what it meant to be truly sad, and so she had a whole new appreciation for joy.

73

"And we wear a smile..."

It might not have seemed real, the power of the smiles that these three robots wore at just that moment, but the smiles *were* real. Each knew the joy of teamwork. They went on with their song —

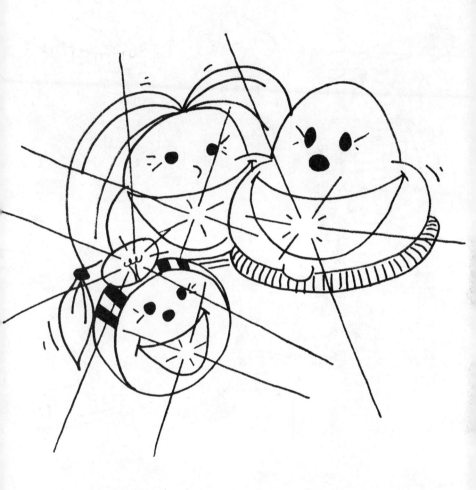

"And we wear a smile just to let the whole world
know that this somebody's happy."

And just then all three robots felt a need to express their individual joy.

Neg sang "Somebody's Happy."

Then Semi-Pos sang "Somebody's Happy."

And Pos sang "Somebody's Happy."

Then, as a team, loud and clear so the whole world could hear them, they sang "Somebody's Happy INSIDE!"

In a month the robots went to the repair station
together. Semi-Pos was fitted with a new arm.

81

Pos received a new leg, and

Neg was fitted with a new neck that worked perfectly.

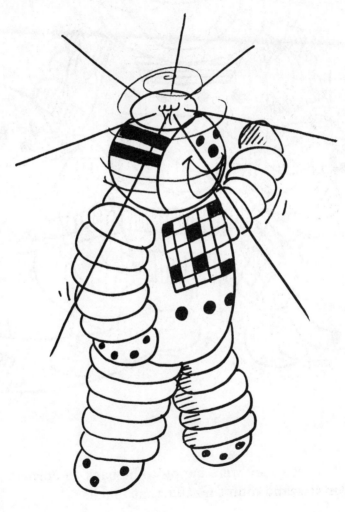

Of course they were happy to be back to normal, but
by then it really didn't matter that much.

They had learned that when they worked together
they could overcome any problem. They learned that
they could live happy wonderful lives if that is what they
wanted.

85

Happiness was really up to them.

Dear Reader,

Are you a "POS" person? To be a "POS" takes a lot of work every day. It is easy to be a "NEG", but it is not a happy way to live your life. A "POS" works harder. When problems come up, and problems do come up every day for all of us, a "POS" takes the positive side and says, "This problem is an opportunity if I make it so".

Look at every hardship as an opportunity to learn, to grow stronger.

Working together as a team will help you in so many ways. First of all there is the joy of sharing. You'll learn to care about others and about what happens in their lives. Next you'll feel the excitement when you see your friends making progress, and when they fail you will benefit even from failure.

The world needs more "POS" people. I hope you'll join the growing number of "POS" people in this world.

Remember, it is your choice. You can be a "POS", a "SEMI-POS", or a "NEG". It is up to you.

> Your "POS" friend,
> Art Fettig

A Dozen "POS" Discussion Starters.

Q. What are some ways that "NEG" and "POS" and "SEMI-POS" supported each other? Can you list five ways?

Q. Why do you think "NEG" was afraid to meet his friends in the park?

Q. What are some ways you support your friends? How do they support you?

Q. What is one reason robots sing their happiness song every day?

Q. What do you think would have happened if the three robots had not worked together?

Q. "POS" learned that it isn't what is wrong that matters, it is how you react to what is wrong. How did "POS" change her attitude?

Q. Share an example of how team work helped you in your life.

Q. What is your favorite part of the Robot song? Why?

Q. What do you think would have happened if "POS" did not have "SEMI-POS" and "NEG" as friends?

Q. What was the real cause of "POS'" unhappiness?

Q. How can you apply the lesson in this book to your own life today? Remember, you might apply the ideas in this book to any problem you may face today.

Q. Do you believe you'd like to be a "POS" person? If you do, then how do you plan to act like a "POS" today?

About the author...

Art Fettig is known as "The Wizard of Pos." He is president of Growth Unlimited, Inc. anorganization dedicated to bringing positive living concepts to parents, children and teachers.

Mr. Fettig believes that high self-esteem is the key to the prevention of problems such as drug abuse, poor grades, teen pregnancies, teen suicides and juvenile crime. His Three Robot Series of books were written expressly for parents to read to their children while they hug them and tell them, "There is greatness in you."

Fettig is the author of 20 books including Pos Parenting-A Guide to Greatness, a book which contains 25 keys for building your child's self-esteem. His book It Only Hurts When I Frown is a funny look at the challenging experience of raising his own four children.

Teachers throughout the United States have used the Three Robot Books in the classroom with great success.

Art Fettig is a professional speaker who gives a hundred speeches and seminars each year to audiences throughout the United States and Canada. He has the rare gift to hold audiences of all ages spellbound as he shares good humor, inspiration and a lot of practical advise on The Art of Positive Living.

He resides with his wife, Ruth, at 31 East Ave. S., Battle Creek, Michigan, 49017 and can be reached at (616) 965-2229

About the artist...

Joe Carpenter has been drawing since he was six years old. When he ran out of paper he drew on the walls and on the furniture. He studied art in Junior High and in High School at Harper Creek School in Battle Creek, Michigan, where his Art teacher, John Roy, recognized his talent and encouraged him.

Joe Carpenter's book publications include The Three Robots, Remembering, The Santa Train, The Three Robots and the Sandstorm, The Three Robots Find A Grandpa, The Three Robots Discover Their Pos-Abilities, The Pos Activity Book, Pos Parenting, How Funny Are You?, The Three Robots Learn About Drugs and the Pos "Just Say Yes!" Activity Book.

One of the outstanding features of Joe Carpenter's work is his artistic inventiveness. Backgrounds abound with loveable animals happily engaged in the joy of living.

Joe Carpenter dedicates his work, with love, to his two daughters, Melissa Ann Carpenter and Felicia Rana Carpenter.

For Children
Books and Tapes that Turn Kids into Winners!

THE THREE ROBOTS — Positive Attitudes — This charming story is the first book of the popular "Pos" series. It follows the adventures of Pos, Semi-Pos, and Neg. From the three robot's experiences, your children discover the true meaning of what it takes to be happy and how to stay that way, to always keep a smile and to make things go their way.

This matching "THREE ROBOTS" Cassette tape makes an excellent bedtime companion for you to share with your children too. Somewhat subliminal in nature, you will actually see a happier child the next morning as a result of listening to the tape the night before.

CH-B1 Book **$3.95**, CH-T1 Tape **$5.95**
CH-B&T1 Book & Tape **$9.90**

THE THREE ROBOTS AND THE SANDSTORM — Overcoming Handicaps · Teamwork — This is the second book of the exciting "POS" series. A continuing tale of the lives and adventures of Pos, Semi-Pos and Neg. This time, the three friends become trapped in a ferocious sandstorm. When it blows over, they find themselves disabled because of the sand in their joints. Their only hope is to make it to the Robot Repair Center. And what will they find out, when they finally make it there?

This story teaches your children the true meaning of friendship and what it takes to remain happy, no matter what difficulty they might ever face.

The matching cassette tape makes for an entertaining after school activity for your children and their friends. Together, they learn the true value of their own friendship and have fun in the process. A very rewarding experience for everyone.

CH-B2 Book **$3.95**, CH-T2 Tape **$5.95**
CH-B&T2 Book & Tape **$9.90**

THE THREE ROBOTS DISCOVER THEIR POS-ABILITIES — Goal Setting — In this adventure, our robot friends discover a successful goal-setting technique. As they apply it, Neg gets a rocket ride, Semi-Pos becomes an aerobic dance instructor and Pos becomes a pop singer and dancer on TV. This book contains a practical goal-setting plan that works for readers of all ages.

CH-B3 Book $3.95, CH-T3 Tape $5.95
CH-B&T3 Book & Tape $9.90

THE THREE ROBOTS FIND A GRANDPA — A Lesson In Love — As we continue the exciting "Pos" series, our three robots, Pos, Semi-Pos, and Neg meet an unhappy, unloved old man who hates everything and everybody, especially Robots. Our friends patiently teach the old man how to become lovable, how to love himself and finally how to love others.

This powerful message is .also available on cassette and by repeated listening, both parents and children may reinforce this concept that will prevent many of the addictions encountered by so many in later years. A message for all to live by.

CH-B4 Book $3.95, CH-T4 Tape $5.95
CH-B&T4 Book & Tape $9.90

THE POS ACTIVITY BOOK — A complete collection of fun ideas and activities for children to enjoy for hours. It is actually an entertaining road map for children to follow. It teaches them positive self-awareness concepts while having fun at the same time. The Pos Activity Book can also be used by teachers and be transformed into a 20-week positive-living course for the classroom.

CH-B5 Activity Book $5.95

REMEMBERING — Memory — There has never been anything like this before. This unique book will actually teach your child how to increase his or her memory, using word association. It accomplishes this through a splendid tale of a boy who thinks he has a broken memory. A kind old man comes along and teaches the boy a fun, easy way of remembering things better.

By imitating the old man's example in the story, your child's memory will begin to improve from the very first day. Parents can benefit from this remarkable memory system too.

CH-B6 Book $3.95, CH-T6 Tape $5.95
CH-B&T6 Book & Tape $9.90

THE THREE ROBOTS LEARN ABOUT DRUGS — In this adventure story The President calls the Three Robots to Washington to help fight the war on alcohol and drugs among our young people. The robots make their own investigation into the problem and come up with some solutions that should help young people learn that they should "Just say no to drugs." Pos contributes her own plan to help involving a crusade to, "Just say yes to positive living."

CH-B7 Book $3.95, CH-T7 Tape $5.95
CH-B&T7 Book & Tape $9.90

THE POS "JUST SAY YES" ACTIVITY BOOK — Based on the poem Just Say Yes, this idea packed activity book goes far beyond the, "Just say no to drugs," concept and provides practical, fun activities that teach positive living, respect for self, concern for others and other character building subjects that will help a child learn to feel good enough about himself or herself to stand up and say no when drugs are offered: Provides material for a 20 week program.

CH-B8 Activity Book $5.95

NOW · POS STICKERS — Kids love to wear stickers on their clothes and to paste them on their books, etc. With a Pos Achievement Card you receive 10 Pos 4-color stickers. Great for encouraging Pos Activities with your children.

CH-ST Sticker Sets $1.25 each
CH-250ST 250"I'm A Pos" Stickers $15.00 per roll

POS PINS — Attractive 4-color Pos-Pins. Children Love Them!

CH-P Pin $1.00 each

TAPES FOR KIDS — Individual tapes of four Three Robots Books, Remembering, plus a special tape for parents on how to get the most out of the 3 Robot Products. All in an attractive album.

CH-A1 $34.95

---

3 Robots Combination Special

6 Books including the Pos Activity Book, 6 Tapes, 10 "I'm A Pos" stickers, 1 Pos Pin and a Pos Achievement Card.

A $63.95 Value for
CH-C1 $49.95

SAVE $14.00

For Parents

"POS" PARENTING — A Guide To Greatness with 25 Keys for Building Your Child's Self-Esteem — A warm, friendly practical look at the importance of attitude and self-esteem and it's importance in living a happy, successful life.

PR-B1 Book $5.95

IT ONLY HURTS WHEN I FROWN — A funny, happy loving look at life. A series of humorous sketches on the author's family relationships while raising four children. Share the joys of homework, dining out, defective cars, parking tickets and much more.

PR-B2 Book $5.95

THE ART OF POSITIVE PARENTING — A delightful 2 tape album recorded live at a parenting seminar featuring Art Fettig.
25 ways to build your child's self-esteem.

PR-A1 Album $20.00

ORDER TODAY

GROWTH UNLIMITED, INC.
31 East Avenue South
Battle Creek, Michigan 49017
(616) 965-2229

Quantity	Item No.		Description	Price Each	Price Total

Subtotal	
Michigan Residents add 4% Sales Tax	
★ Shipping and Handling	$2.00
Total	

Indicate Method of Payment Below:
☐ Enclosed (check or money order)
☐ MASTER CHARGE

The Number above your name

and Account Number (all digits)

☐ VISA/BANKAMERICARD
  Account Number (all digits)

☐ AMERICAN EXPRESS
  Account Number (all digits)

Signature _____
Charge Card Expires:

Month _____ Year _____

Phone
Number (   ) _____

Ship To: (Please Print)

NAME _____

ADDRESS _____

CITY _____

STATE _____ ZIP _____